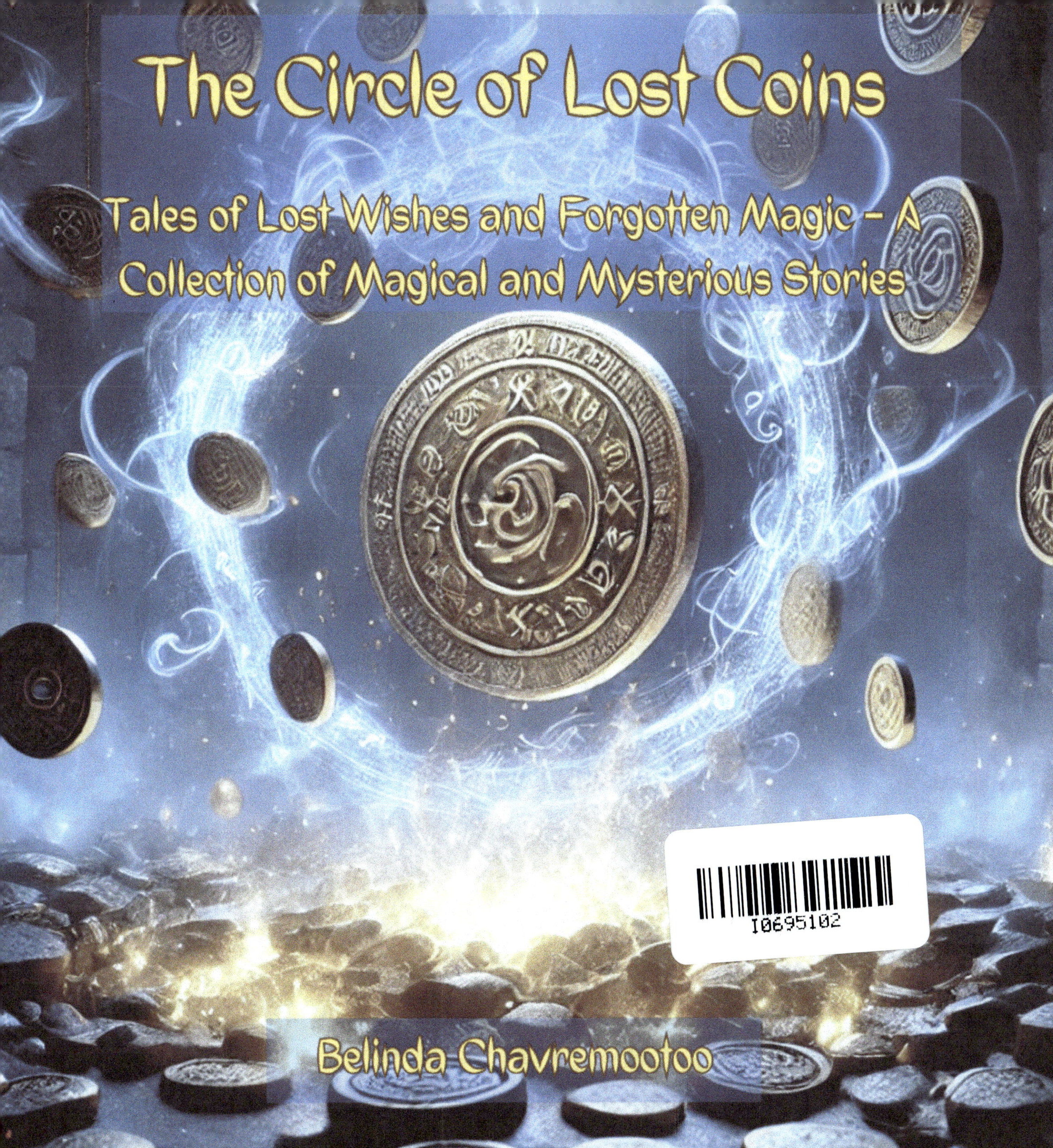

The Circle of Lost Coins
Tales of Lost Wishes and Forgotten Magic – A
Collection of Magical and Mysterious Stories
Belinda Chavremootoo

The Circle of Lost Coins
Tales of Lost Wishes and Forgotten Magic - A
Collection of Magical and Mysterious Stories

This treasured book belongs to

Table of Contents

AUTHOR'S NOTE

Some coins hold more than just value—they hold stories, memories, and wishes waiting to be found.

I have always been fascinated by the idea that every coin passes through countless hands, across time and distance. Each one has a history. A wish someone made. A moment that mattered.

That idea sparked *The Circle of Lost Coins*—a collection of stories about magic, mystery, and the power of remembering. Whether it's a ghostly whisper, a wish too powerful, or a coin that vanishes and reappears, each story reminds us that the past is never truly lost.

Maybe you've held a coin and wondered where it has been. Maybe you've made a wish and waited for it to come true. Maybe, just maybe, there's a little bit of magic in the things we leave behind.

Thank you for stepping into this world of lost wishes and forgotten stories. **What would you do if you found a coin that whispered back?**

Keep dreaming. Keep wondering. Keep searching for magic.

Belinda Chavremootoo

The Ghost Coins

An eerie and emotional mystery in an ancient marketplace

The Market of Lost Things

Theo loved the marketplace.

It was **old, loud, and filled with stories**. Every stall had something strange—jewelry that didn't match, books missing their covers, clocks that didn't tick.

Theo called it **The Market of Lost Things**.

"People say some things here don't want to be found," his grandmother warned.
Theo **rolled his eyes**. "You mean ghosts?"

His grandmother only smiled. "Not all ghosts are the kind you see."

Theo didn't believe in ghosts. But that was before he found **the coin**.

It happened at a small, dusty stall tucked in the farthest corner of the market.

The old merchant was sorting through a wooden box, his fingers brushing over **odd, mismatched coins**. Some were rusted. Some were gold.

And one…
One looked **ordinary**.
Just a penny.

But as soon as Theo's eyes landed on it, his stomach **twisted**. It was **colder** than the other coins.

Darker.

And when the merchant lifted it, it made a sound that sent a chill down Theo's spine.

Like a sigh.

Theo shook the feeling off. "How much for that one?"

The merchant **hesitated**.
"That one?" His fingers tightened around the coin. "That one always comes back."

Theo **laughed**. "A coin can't be haunted!"

The merchant **didn't laugh**.
But he let Theo take it.

And that night, as Theo lay in bed, he felt something cold against his fingers.

The penny.

Even though he had spent it at another stall.

Even though it should be **gone**.

The Whisper in the Dark

Theo stared at the penny in his hand.

No. This isn't possible.

He had spent it. At the bakery stall.
He had **watched** the merchant drop it into the cash tin.
But now… it was **back**.
Colder than before. Darker than before.
And just as Theo was about to throw it across the room —

A whisper filled the air.

"I was forgotten… I was lost…"

Theo froze. His heart **pounded**.
The room was **completely dark**. Completely silent.
Except for that whisper.
It wasn't coming from outside.
It wasn't coming from the wind.

It was coming from the penny.

A Voice from the Past

Theo's breath hitched.

No. No way.

Coins didn't talk. Coins didn't **whisper**. He gripped the penny **tightly** in his fist. The coldness **spread** through his fingers.

"I was forgotten… I was lost…"

Theo **threw the coin onto his desk**.

I'm imagining things. It's just a stupid old penny.

He squeezed his eyes shut. Pulled the blankets over his head. But the whisper **returned**. Softer. **Sadder**.

"Please… don't forget me too."

Theo's eyes snapped open. His hands **shook**.
For the first time, he wasn't so sure he didn't believe in ghosts.

The Forgotten Wish

Theo didn't sleep. The penny **stayed on his desk**, silent now.
But the whisper still **echoed in his mind**.

"Please… don't forget me too."

The next morning, Theo was done with this. He grabbed the
penny and **marched back to the market**. He would return it.
He would toss it. **Anything to get rid of it**. But when he
reached the old merchant's stall —

The merchant was gone.
The stall was **empty**. Like it had never been there at all.
Theo's fingers tightened around the penny. Rust flaked off at
his touch.

And the whisper came again.
"I made a wish once…"

Theo **shuddered**.
What wish?
Who are you?
And deep down, he already knew — **He had to find out**.

Searching for the Lost Story

Theo didn't go home.
I made a wish once…

The whisper **wouldn't leave his mind**. The market was **alive with voices**, but Theo wasn't listening. He needed answers. His eyes landed on an **old storyteller** sitting near the spice stalls. A man who had spent his life collecting **forgotten tales**.
Theo hurried over. "Sir, do you know about a boy who worked in the market long ago?"
The old man **tilted his head**.
Then—slowly—he nodded.
"A long time ago," he said, "there was a boy who used to sell newspapers here."
Theo leaned in. "What happened to him?"
The old man's expression **darkened**.
"No one knows. He was here one day… and gone the next."
Theo's hands tightened around the penny.

Was this his coin?

The old man sighed. "But before he disappeared, they say… he made a wish."

The Wish That Was Never Heard

Theo's heart raced.
A boy who disappeared...
A wish that was never answered...

The old storyteller **sighed**.
"They say he stood right here, in the middle of the market, and tossed a coin into the air."
Theo's fingers **tightened** around the penny.

This coin.

"But before the coin landed," the old man continued, "a strong wind came."
"It swept the coin away."

The wish was never made.
It was never heard.

Theo **stared** at the coin in his hand.
"*Please... don't forget me too.*"
The voice was clearer now.
The boy wasn't haunting the coin.
The coin was haunting the boy.

A Wish Waiting to Be Made

Theo's hands **shook**.
The coin didn't just belong to the boy…
It was carrying his unfinished wish.

Silvy, the smart penny from the Circle of Pennies, would have
known what to do. The Circle of Pennies **granted lost wishes**.
But Theo was just a kid. How could he help a ghost?
He looked down at the coin.
It felt **warmer now**.
Like it was **waiting**.
Theo took a slow breath.
And for the first time, he listened.

A whisper filled his mind.
A boy's voice, small and hopeful.
"I wish… I wish someone would remember me."

Theo's chest **tightened**.

That was the wish?
To not be forgotten?
And in that moment, Theo knew— It wasn't too late.

The Wishkeeper's Light

The market was **buzzing with life**.
But to Theo, it felt like time **had stopped**.
He stared at the coin, feeling the weight of a wish that was
never heard.

I can fix this.

Theo stepped forward, back to where the old storyteller said
the boy had been.
He gripped the coin **tightly** in his palm.
Took a deep breath.
And whispered—

"I remember you."

A wind rushed through the marketplace.
The coin in his hand grew warm.
Glowed **softly**.
Theo felt something **shift**.
Like a door opening.
Like a story **finally finishing**.

Setting the Wish Free

The wind **swirled** around Theo.
The coin **glowed brighter**.

Something's happening…

The whisper **wasn't sad anymore**.
It was **strong**. Clear.

"Thank you."

Theo's chest **tightened**.
He took a deep breath.
And with all his heart, he whispered—

"Your wish is heard."

The glow **flashed**.
A soft, golden light **rose from the coin… then faded into
the air**.
Theo **watched in silence**.
And for the first time since he found the coin…
The whisper **was gone**.

No More Whispers

The wind **settled**. The glow **disappeared**.
Theo stood in the middle of the marketplace, staring at the coin in his hand. It felt **warm now**. Normal. Like any other coin.

The wish was heard.

Theo exhaled, his heart feeling… **lighter**.
The old storyteller watched him from his stall, a small smile on his lips. "You did something special today," he said.
Theo didn't answer. He simply looked up at the sky… and for the briefest moment—
He thought he heard a voice in the wind. "**Thank you.**"
Theo smiled. Then, he **flipped the penny into the air**.
It spun once. Twice. And when it landed, it stayed **right where it was**.
No more whispers.
No more ghosts.
Just a penny.
A penny, and a story **finally complete**.

*** The End ***

The Chamber of Lost Wishes

A hidden vault holding the most dangerous, powerful wishes
ever made

The Hidden Door

Eli loved the underground tunnels.
He loved how they twisted and turned beneath the old town,
like they were hiding stories no one else remembered.
But Eli didn't feel like he belonged up there—in the town with
all the noise, the crowds, and the kids who didn't notice him.
Down here? In the tunnels? He felt **like someone special**.

One day, as he wandered deeper than ever before, he saw
something that made him stop.
It was a **door**, carved into the stone wall.
Eli blinked.
It wasn't like any door he'd ever seen. It had **no handle, no
keyhole—just a small coin slot in the center**.
Symbols swirled across the surface, glowing faintly as if they'd
been waiting for someone to find them.
Eli's heart **pounded**.
"What is this?" he whispered, reaching out to trace the
carvings. The stone was **warm to the touch**.
Then he noticed the words etched above the coin slot:

For the kind of
heart,
the forgotten
shall reveal their
secrets

38

"For the kind of heart, the forgotten shall reveal their secrets."

Eli tilted his head. "The kind of heart? What does that mean?"
He pulled out a few coins from his pocket—a shiny new penny,
a silver quarter, and an old rusty coin he'd found by the market
earlier. He tried the shiny penny first. The coin **slipped in**—and
nothing happened. The quarter clinked inside—still, nothing.

Finally, Eli picked up the rusty old coin.
It felt **different in his hand—heavier, warmer**.
When he dropped it into the slot—

The door **rumbled**.

The carvings glowed brighter, the symbols swirling like golden
mist. Slowly, the door **creaked open**. Eli's breath caught.
Behind the door was a chamber, glowing softly with golden
light. And inside…

Millions of coins, whispering, floating, waiting.

Eli stepped forward.
He didn't know it yet, but he was about to change everything.

The Vault of Wishes

Eli stepped inside.
The chamber was **massive**, stretching farther than his eyes could see.
And the coins…

They floated.
They glowed.
They whispered.

Eli's breath caught in his throat.
Some coins shimmered like **fireflies**, blinking in and out of sight. Others hummed softly, sending ripples of golden light through the air.

And some…
Some just **sat there**, silent, as if they had forgotten how to shine.
Eli **shivered**.

What is this place?

His footsteps echoed as he walked deeper into the vault.

The air **felt heavy**—like the room was holding its breath.
Then, he saw it.

A coin.
Not floating. Not glowing.
Just sitting in the middle of the chamber, waiting.

Something **pulled** at Eli's chest.
Slowly, carefully, he reached for it.

The ground trembled beneath him.

A deep voice filled the air.

"Who dares awaken a forgotten wish?"

Eli's eyes widened in terror.

I think I just made a huge mistake.

The Wishkeeper's Warning

The ground **shook**.
The walls **rippled like water**.

Eli **stumbled back**, clutching the coin in his hand.
From the shadows, something **moved**.

A figure stepped forward—tall, cloaked in golden mist.
Its voice echoed all around him.

"You have entered the Chamber of Lost Wishes."
"And you have taken what was meant to be forgotten."

Eli's heart **pounded**.

The door… I need to get to the door…

But when he turned, the entrance was **gone**.
Only endless rows of **floating coins remained**.

The figure stepped closer.

Eli could barely breathe.

"Who… who are you?" he whispered.

The figure's eyes **glowed softly**.

"I am the Wishkeeper. The guardian of forgotten wishes."

"Only those with a kind heart can enter this place."

"That is why the door let you in."

Eli gripped the coin **tighter**.

Then why does it feel like I just did something really, really wrong?

A Choice with Consequences

Eli's fingers tightened around the coin.
The Wishkeeper watched him, its golden eyes **calm but unyielding**.

"Do you know what you hold?"

Eli swallowed.
He looked down at the coin in his palm.
It was **old, worn, and cracked**.
But unlike the others, it didn't glow.
It didn't whisper.

Why does this one feel... different?

Eli shook his head. "I—I don't know."

The Wishkeeper **sighed**.

"Some wishes were lost for a reason."
"Some were too powerful."
"Some… were never meant to be granted."

Eli's stomach **dropped**.
He looked at the coin again.
There was **an inscription, half-faded**.
A wish that had been started… but never finished.

"If you speak the final words, the wish will come true," the
Wishkeeper said.
"But beware—wishes have consequences."

The room **hummed**. The other coins floated around him, as
if waiting to see what he would do.

Do I finish the wish?
Or put it back before it's too late?

Eli's heart **raced**.
And then—
He **whispered the final words**.

A Wish That Changes Everything

Eli's voice **barely left his lips**.
But the moment the final words were spoken—
The chamber exploded with golden light.
The coins **whirled around him, spinning faster and faster.**
The Wishkeeper's cloak **flared like fire**.
Eli **shielded his eyes**. "What's happening?!"

"You finished a wish that was never meant to be," the
Wishkeeper's voice boomed.

The air shimmered.
The room shifted.

Something was changing.

Eli blinked against the light, and suddenly—
He wasn't in the chamber anymore.
He was **somewhere else**.
Somewhere he **recognized**.
Somewhere he **never thought he'd see again.**

The World That Shouldn't Exist

Eli's breath **hitched.**
The golden light faded. And suddenly—**he was standing in a place he knew… but also didn't**.
It was his town. The same winding streets. The same market stalls. The same **sky**. But something was **wrong**.

Everything looked… new.

The stone buildings weren't cracked and worn.
The trees weren't gnarled with age.
The people walking past weren't rushing—**they were smiling, laughing, untouched by time.**
Eli's hands **shook**. "This isn't real…"
Then he heard it.

A voice—soft, familiar.
"Eli…?"

His heart stopped. Slowly, he turned. And standing there, staring at him with wide, **disbelieving eyes**—
Was someone he never thought he'd see again.

MARKETPLAC

The Face from the Past

Eli's heart pounded.
The person standing before him… **shouldn't be here.**
He was supposed to be **gone**.
Lost.
A memory **fading with time**.
But now—
He was real.
Breathing.
Looking at him like he was the one who didn't belong.

I made the wish come true.

The world around him **felt heavier**.
Too perfect.
Too bright.
The wish **was changing everything**.
And Eli finally realized—

Not all wishes are meant to be granted.

MARKETPLAC

A Wish Too Powerful

Eli took a shaky breath.
The world around him **looked perfect**—but it felt **wrong**.
Too clean. Too golden. Too still.
And the person standing before him?
He was not supposed to be here.

I wished for something that should've stayed lost.

The person—**someone Eli had once loved and lost**—
stepped closer.
"Eli… why do you look so scared?"

Eli **couldn't answer**.
Because deep down, he knew the truth.

The world had shifted.
The past had been rewritten.
And now, time itself was unraveling.

When Time Breaks

Eli's mind spun.

This was a mistake.

The world around him **looked perfect**.
The town was **brighter, untouched by time**.
The people smiled, **unaware that something was wrong**.
And Finn…
Finn was **standing right in front of him**.

Eli's breath caught.
His twin brother **looked exactly as he remembered**.
Messy hair. Bright eyes. The same mischievous smile.
Finn **didn't change**.
But Eli did.

Finn grinned. **"Why do you look like you've seen a ghost?"**
Eli opened his mouth, but no words came out.

Because you are one.

Finn just **laughed** and grabbed Eli's arm.
"Come on, slowpoke! We still have to race to the big tree!"
Eli's stomach **twisted**.

We used to race all the time.
Before…

He swallowed hard. "Finn, wait—"
But Finn was already running ahead, **just like he always did**.
Like nothing had changed.
Like no time had passed at all.

But it had.

Eli took a shaky breath—
And followed.

The Only Way Out

Eli followed Finn through the glowing town.
His heart pounded.

This isn't real.

But Finn—**laughing, running, completely alive—felt real.
Too real**.

"Come on!" Finn called over his shoulder. "You're so slow
now!"
Eli's breath hitched.
He used to be the slow one.
But now…

I've grown up. And Finn hasn't.

They reached the big tree in the town square.
Finn skidded to a stop, **grinning**.

SHOP

"You finally caught up!"
Eli didn't answer.
Because something **caught his eye**.
In the shop window beside them—

Their reflection.

Eli's chest **tightened**.
His own face was **older**.
Finn's wasn't.
Finn noticed Eli staring.
His grin **faded**.
He looked at his own hands.
His small, unchanged hands.
Slowly, his fingers curled into a fist.
He swallowed hard.

He knows.

Finn turned to Eli.
"How long was I gone?"

SHOP

The Undoing of a Wish

Eli's throat tightened.
Finn's question **hung in the air**.
"How long was I gone?"
Eli **couldn't answer**.
His hands shook.

How do you tell your twin brother that he's been gone for years? That he drowned? That you couldn't save him?

Finn looked down at himself.
At his small hands.
At the unchanged world around him.
His breath hitched.
His voice was quieter now.
"I didn't grow up, did I?"
Eli's chest **ached**.
He shook his head. **"No."**
Finn exhaled **slowly**.
For the first time, his smile **faltered**.

The town around them **shimmered**.
Shadows stretched **in the wrong direction**.
Buildings flickered between **past and present**.
The air filled with whispers.

"Some wishes must remain lost…"

"Time cannot be rewritten…"

"Let go."

Finn's hands trembled.
He looked at Eli.
At the town breaking apart around them.

He understands now.

His voice wavered.
"I was never supposed to stay, was I?"
Eli's eyes burned. **"No."**

Finn swallowed hard.
Then—he **smiled.**
"It's okay, Eli."

Eli's breath hitched.

How can he be okay with this?

How can I?

Finn **reached out**—his small fingers curling around Eli's.
"You don't have to keep searching for me."
"I was always with you."

The world **shook.**
Golden cracks **split through the sky.**
Finn's body **began to fade.**
"Goodbye, Eli."

A Wish Remembered

Eli **reached for Finn**—but his fingers only touched air.
Finn's smile **remained**, even as the golden light **pulled him away**.
Eli's chest **ached**.

I don't want to let go.

But he had to.
And so—he did.

The world **shattered**.
The golden town **collapsed into light**.
The whispers **faded**.

And when Eli opened his eyes—
He was back in the tunnels.

The **Chamber of Lost Wishes** was gone.

No golden glow.
No floating coins.
Just silence.
Eli's fingers brushed his pocket.

Empty.

The coin was gone, too.
Like it had never been there at all.

But something inside him **felt different**.
Lighter.
Like he had carried something heavy for a long time—
And finally let it go.

The next morning, Eli walked through the town.
The **real town**.
It wasn't golden. It wasn't perfect.
But it was **home**.
He passed by the market, the streets, the places that once
felt too big for him.

And when he looked up at the sky—
He whispered a wish.

Not to change the past.

Not to bring back what was lost.

But to always remember.

And as he turned to leave—
The wind whispered back.

*** The End ***

The Coin That Fell from the Stars

A magical and inspirational story about wishes, belonging, and the universe

The Falling Light

Nova talked to the stars.

Not out loud, of course—she wasn't weird.

But when she lay on her rooftop at night, staring at the endless sky, she felt like they were **listening**.
Like they were **watching over her**.
Like they were **the only ones who understood**.

She would whisper her thoughts, and they would blink in response.

"Today was hard." (A soft twinkle.)
 "I wonder if people really change." (A flicker in the distance.)
 "Do you think my parents would be proud of me?" (A sudden, unexpected shimmer.)

The stars never spoke, but they **agreed** with her.

That night, the sky felt **different**.
The air was **still**.
The stars **hushed, waiting**.
Then—

A silver streak cut across the darkness.

A shooting star.
Nova sat up. "That was—"
But before she could finish, the light changed direction.

It wasn't falling like a normal star—it was coming down.

Straight toward the woods beyond her house.

That's not normal.

Her heart pounded.

She scrambled down from the roof, grabbed a flashlight, and
ran toward the trees.

The woods were **quiet**. Too quiet.
Nova's breath **fogged the air** as she stepped carefully over fallen leaves. She followed the silver glow, deeper and deeper —until she saw it.
Not a meteor. Not a piece of space rock.
A coin.
Lying in the grass, **glowing softly**.
Nova **stared**.

What kind of star falls as a coin?

She reached out, hesitating.
Then—**she picked it up**.

The moment her fingers touched the surface, the stars above her shifted.
As if the whole universe had just **taken a breath**.
Nova's pulse **raced**.

This… this isn't just a coin.

It was **something else**.
Something **waiting to be found**.
And Nova had just become **part of its story**.

The Whisper of the Cosmos

The coin **hummed** in Nova's palm.
Not a loud hum—just a soft, steady pulse.
Like a quiet heartbeat.
Like it was… **alive**.
Nova swallowed hard.

This isn't normal.

She turned it over, expecting to see some kind of writing, but
— Nothing.
No numbers. No symbols.
Just smooth, glowing metal that **shouldn't exist**.
That night, Nova sat on her rooftop again, the coin resting
beside her.
The stars above flickered, **as if they knew**.
She took a deep breath.

"Where did you come from?"

The coin didn't answer.
But the air around her **shifted**.
The stars seemed to **lean closer**.
Then—

A whisper.

Not a voice.
Not words.
A feeling.
Soft. Ancient. Searching.

"A wish once made... never truly fades."

Nova's heart **pounded**.

Did I just hear that... or feel it?

She looked at the coin.
It **glowed** a little brighter.
Like it had been waiting for someone to listen.

The Star Map

Nova couldn't sleep.
The coin sat on her desk, **glowing faintly in the dark**.

"A wish once made… never truly fades."

The words **echoed** in her mind.
What wish?
Whose wish?

She sat up, grabbed the coin, and held it under the
moonlight. That's when she saw them.
Tiny, **almost invisible markings** appeared on the surface—
like delicate **cracks in the metal**. No… not cracks.

A map.

The lines curved, twisted—**forming constellations**.
Nova's breath **caught**.
This wasn't just a coin.
It was a message.
A map written in **starlight**.
And it was leading her **somewhere**.

The Observatory's Secret

Nova traced the glowing lines on the coin.
A **map written in starlight**.
But where did it lead?
She grabbed her phone and pulled up a star chart.
Her fingers moved quickly—matching the coin's markings
to constellations.
And then—

A perfect match.

The map was pointing to a **real place**.
The abandoned observatory on the edge of town.

The next night, Nova stood in front of the old observatory.
It was dark. Quiet. **Forgotten**. She hesitated.

If I go inside, there's no turning back.

The coin in her pocket hummed. Like it was encouraging
her. Nova took a deep breath—
And stepped inside.

The Celestial Book

The observatory smelled like **dust and forgotten time**.
Nova's flashlight cut through the darkness, revealing **rusted telescopes** and stacks of old books.
The air **felt charged**, like the whole place was waiting. Then—
Her light landed on something strange. A **pedestal**.
And on top of it…
A book.

Nova's hands **trembled** as she lifted the cover.
Inside, there were **no words**.
Just **star charts, swirling constellations, and strange symbols**.
But one page **stood out**.
A single wish, written in a language she couldn't understand—
except for one line.

"To find the lost ones and bring them home."

Nova's pulse raced. She reached into her pocket—the coin was glowing brighter than ever.
Somehow, she knew—
This book held the answer.

The Cosmic Doorway

Nova's fingers traced the words.

"To find the lost ones and bring them home."

Her heart **pounded**.

Who made this wish?
And who are the lost ones?

The coin in her pocket **hummed, warmer now**.

Like it had been waiting for this moment.
Then—

The observatory trembled.

The air around her **shifted**.
One of the walls—no, **not a wall... a door**.
A door that **hadn't been there before**.

And in the center of it—

A slot, the **exact size of her coin**.

Nova's breath **shook**.

She pulled out the coin.
It glowed like a **tiny piece of a star**.

Do I do this?
Do I open the door?

Her hands **trembled**—but she knew the answer.

She lifted the coin—
And slid it into the slot.

The entire room exploded with light.

The Message from the Stars

Nova squeezed her eyes shut.
The **light** was too bright, too powerful—like she was standing inside a star.
Then, as suddenly as it appeared— It **vanished**.
Nova blinked.
The observatory was **gone**.
She was standing in an endless sky.

Floating. Weightless. Suspended among the stars.

A soft **hum** filled the air.
She turned—
And gasped.
A **figure made of stardust** stood before her.
It had no face, no mouth—just two glowing lights where its eyes should be.
Then—
It **spoke**.

"You have answered our call."

Nova's breath **hitched**.

Whose call?
Who are you?

The figure lifted a hand, and suddenly—

Memories flooded into her mind.

Stars **burning out**.
Voices **calling across galaxies**.

A wish, made long ago—
"To find the lost ones and bring them home."

Nova staggered back.
She finally understood.

The wish… it wasn't for Earth.
It was for them.

The Forgotten Travellers

Nova's mind **spun**.

The memories rushing through her weren't hers—
They belonged to **them**.

The lost ones.

She saw flashes of **golden ships drifting through space.**
Planets abandoned.
Stars dimming. And then—**darkness.**

A voice whispered, soft but aching:

"We have been searching… for so long."

Nova's breath **caught**.

They're not just lost.
They've been waiting.

She looked down—**the coin in her hand flickered**.

Not as a message.
Not as a map.
As a beacon.

The wish was never about **finding a place**.

It was about **finding each other**.

Nova swallowed hard.

"How do I help you?"

The stardust figure lifted a hand—
And pointed to the **sky**.

The Final Wish

Nova followed the figure's gaze.
Above them, the stars **shifted**. The constellations **realigned**.
And in the vast emptiness of space—
A path appeared.

The way home.

The figure turned back to her.

"You are the final piece."

Nova's heart **pounded**.
She looked down at the coin, **glowing softly in her palm**.
It had always been **waiting** for the right person.
Someone to **hear the call**. Someone to **complete the wish**.
Nova took a deep breath.
She lifted the coin—
And whispered:
"Find your way home."

The moment the words left her lips—
The universe itself responded.

The Light Returns Home

The coin **glowed brighter than ever**.
Nova **released it**.
It floated upward—**slowly at first, then faster**.
The stars above **rippled**.

The path home had opened.

The stardust figure turned to her.

"Thank you, dreamer."

The form **began to fade**, dissolving into light.

But Nova didn't feel **loss**.
She felt **completion**.
The wish had been granted.

And somewhere, far beyond Earth, the lost ones were
going home.

The light **swallowed her whole**.
And when she opened her eyes—
She was back.
Lying on her rooftop.
The observatory, the glowing door, the coin—**all gone**.
Had it been real?
Nova wasn't sure.
But as she looked up, she saw something **she knew wasn't there before**.
A **new constellation**.
Shaped like a coin, glowing softly.
Like a reminder.
Like a whisper.
Like a **thank you**.
Nova smiled.
And for the first time, she didn't just feel like the stars were listening.

She felt like they knew her name.

*** The End ***

The Vanishing Coin

A magical mystery about things we lose, things we forget, and the things that find their way back

The Coin That Wouldn't Stay Lost

Max wasn't the kind of kid who believed in magic.
Luck? Coincidence? Sure. But magic? **Not a chance**.

So when he found an old coin on the sidewalk after school, he didn't think much of it.
It was **worn and scratched**, with strange markings around the edges.

Max shrugged, flipped it in the air—

CLINK.

Caught it.
Shoved it into his pocket.
And **forgot about it**.

That night, as he emptied his pockets onto his desk, **the coin was gone.**
Max frowned.
He checked his backpack. His pockets. The floor.

Weird...

But whatever. It was just a coin.

The next day, Max was walking past the old library when something **shiny caught his eye**.

A coin.
Lying on the steps.
He bent down and picked it up.

No way...

It was **the same coin**.

The same markings. The same scratches.

Max's stomach **twisted**.

He knew he'd lost this coin.
So why had it **found him again**?

The Coin's Past

Max turned the coin over in his palm.
It looked **ordinary**.
But it **wasn't**.
He had **lost it**.
And now, it was **back**.

This isn't normal.

Max shoved the coin into his pocket—**tighter this time**.

At home, he sat at his desk, laptop open.

If this coin kept **vanishing and reappearing**, then maybe…
maybe it had a story.

He searched for **coins with strange markings**.
Scrolled past **ancient currency, collector's items, pirate treasure**.
And then— A **match**.

An old newspaper clipping from almost **a hundred years ago**.

"The Magician's Missing Coin: A Mystery That Never Ends."

Max's pulse **raced**.

The article told the story of a **famous magician** who performed an impossible trick—

He made a coin disappear... and it never came back.

Until now.

Max looked down at the coin in his hand.

What if this isn't just a coin?

What if it's still looking for something?

The Clues in the Disappearance

Max couldn't stop thinking about the article.

A magician's missing coin?
A trick that never ended?

He turned the coin in his fingers.
If this was **the same coin**, then why was it showing up **now**?
He decided to test it.
That night, he placed the coin on his desk.

He took a picture.
He left the room.
He came back an hour later.
The coin was gone.

Max's heart raced.
He searched the floor. His pockets. The desk.

Vanished.

But the real question was—
Where would it appear next?

The Forgotten Places

Max didn't have to wait long.
The next day, as he walked past the old library—

There it was.

Sitting on the steps.
Waiting.
His stomach **tightened**.

Why here?

He picked it up, turning it over in his fingers.
Then he looked up at the library.
It was **quiet**, almost empty.

Through the window, he saw an **elderly woman** stacking books.
Something about her seemed… **lonely**.
Like she was **a part of the library that everyone had forgotten**.

Max hesitated.
Then, gripping the coin, he stepped inside.

The Librarian's Lost Story

The library smelled like **dust and old paper**.
Max hesitated, clutching the coin.
The elderly librarian looked up, adjusting her glasses.

"Can I help you, dear?"

Max swallowed. "Uh… do you know anything about magic coins?"
Her eyes **narrowed**.
For a moment, she said nothing.
Then she sighed.

"Not all magic is about tricks, you know."
She tapped the desk.
"Some things disappear because people forget them."

Max frowned. *"Like what?"*
The librarian **gave a sad smile**.
"Like stories that were never told."
She motioned to the **dusty section in the back—books untouched for years.** Max's heart **pounded**.

The coin led me here for a reason.

The Vanishing Trick

Max followed the librarian's gaze to the **dusty shelves in the back.**
Books **untouched**. Forgotten.
Just like the coin.

Is this what it's looking for?

He ran his fingers along the spines until he saw it—

An old journal, tucked behind the others.

He pulled it out.
The cover was faded, the pages yellowed.
Inside, in elegant handwriting, was a name.

Elias the Great—The Magician Who Vanished.

Max's breath caught.

This magician…
He's the one who lost the coin.

And now, the coin had found his **story**.

The Magician's Secret

Max flipped through the pages

Elias the Great.
A magician famous for **one impossible trick**.
A trick **no one could explain**. The **Vanishing Coin**.
The journal told the story of a man who had searched for
something **his whole life**.
- He performed in grand theaters.
- He amazed audiences.
- But his final trick was **never an illusion**. One night, during a
  show, he made a coin **disappear**.

And it never came back.
Until now. Max's fingers tightened around the coin.
But why did it return… to me?

The last page of the journal held only **one sentence**.
"The coin will always find what has been forgotten."
Max's stomach **dropped**.

Then what am I supposed to remember?

The Forgotten Trick

Max stared at the journal.

"The coin will always find what has been forgotten."
But what does that mean?

He looked down at the coin. It **shimmered softly**, almost like it was **waiting**. Then—**it vanished**.
Right in front of him.

Max's heart **pounded**. He didn't even feel it leave his hand.
It was just… **gone**.
But if the coin was looking for something forgotten—
Where would it go next?
Max thought back to the librarian. To the books no one read.
To the magician's last trick.

Elias the Great didn't just make a coin disappear.
He was searching for something.

And suddenly, Max knew where to look.

138

The Magician's Final Clue

Max **ran**. Through the library doors. Down the empty streets.
He **knew** where the coin would be.
Not in some random place. Not in a pocket or under his bed.

It was looking for something forgotten.

And there was one place in town where **forgotten things always ended up**. The **old theater**.
Dusty. Boarded up. **Abandoned for years**.
But once, it had been the most **magical** place in town.
And Elias the Great had performed his **final show** here.
Max stepped forward, **his heart pounding**.

If the coin is here… then I'm about to find out why it came back.

He pushed open the creaky doors—
And right there, in the center of the empty stage—

The coin.

Waiting. For him.

The Last Vanishing Act

Max stepped onto the stage.
The air was **thick with dust and silence.**
But the coin sat there, **shining like it had been waiting all these years.**
Max slowly reached for it—
And the moment his fingers touched the surface...
A voice whispered through the empty theater.

"You found me."

Max **froze**. The voice was **soft, distant**—like an echo of something long past.
Then, he saw it. A **faint outline** in the dust, the shape of a man standing in the spotlight.
Elias the Great. The magician who vanished.
The magician who had **lost something he could never find.**
And now, Max understood.

The coin wasn't meant to be owned.
It was meant to complete the trick.
To finish what had been left undone.

Max closed his eyes.
Held the coin tightly one last time—
And whispered:

"Time to go home."

The coin **vanished**.
This time, for good.
And the voice in the theater?

"Thank you."

The next day, Max checked his pockets.
The coin was gone.
For the first time, **it hadn't come back**.
But as he walked past the old theater...
He swore he saw a **faint shimmer of light** on the empty stage.
Like a trick finally finished.
Like a story finally told.
Max smiled.
And walked away.

*** The End ***

The Emperor's Last Coin

A historical mystery about power, legacy, and the weight of the past.

The Unearthed Treasure

Kai wiped the sweat from his forehead.
The sun **blazed down** on the excavation site, turning the dirt beneath his feet into **hot dust**.
He wasn't an archaeologist—**not yet, anyway**.
But spending the summer on a real dig? Helping uncover the lost history of the **Golden Emperor**?

This was the kind of adventure he had always dreamed of.

"Kai! Over here!"

He turned to see **Dr. Lin**, the lead archaeologist, waving him over.
Kai hurried toward her, careful not to step on anything important.
She pointed at a small, **sealed chamber** they had just uncovered.

"We found something."

Inside the chamber, half-buried in dust, lay an **ornate gold chest**.
Kai's heart **pounded**.
Dr. Lin carefully pried it open—
And inside, among the relics and jewels, sat **a single coin**.
Unlike the others, it was **darker, older, different**.

Kai reached for it—

The moment his fingers touched the surface, a whisper filled the air.

"Do not take what belongs to the past."

Kai **staggered back**.

Did anyone else hear that?!

But Dr. Lin was too busy inspecting the other treasures.
Only Kai had heard it.
And in his palm, the coin **felt warm**.
Like it wasn't just metal.
Like it was **alive**.

The Curse of the Forgotten

That night, Kai couldn't sleep.
The ancient coin **sat on his desk**, glowing faintly in the dim light.
It wasn't supposed to be special—just another artifact.
So why did it feel **different**?

And why did it whisper?

Kai turned it over in his fingers.

There were **symbols engraved along the edge**—but the writing was old, **too worn to read**.

His laptop was open beside him, research tabs cluttering the screen.

He had read about **burial curses**, about how emperors were entombed with treasures to ward off thieves.
But this coin wasn't buried with gold.

It had been locked away **alone**.

Suddenly—

A breeze swept through his room.

Kai **froze**.
The windows were **closed**.
But the curtains **fluttered**.
And then—
A shadow **moved** across his wall.
Kai's breath **caught**.

I'm not alone.

He turned sharply—
But there was **no one there**.
Just the coin.
Still **sitting on his desk**.
Still **watching**.

The Emperor's Final Wish

Kai didn't tell anyone about the whisper. Or the shadow.
Or the fact that the coin felt **heavier now**—like it was carrying
something **more than metal**.

It's just my imagination… right?

At breakfast, he pulled out his phone and typed:
Ancient Emperor's Curses – Real or Fake?
He scrolled past myths, legends, and ghost stories until he
found something that made his stomach twist.

The Golden Emperor's Final Wish.

According to legend, the emperor's **last words** were never
recorded. Some say he left a wish behind—one so powerful, it
had to be hidden. And those who tried to uncover it?
They disappeared.
Kai's hand tightened around the coin.
Was this… his last wish?

And if it was— **Was it ever meant to be found?**

The Ghost of the Throne

Kai needed answers.
And he knew exactly where to find them.

That afternoon, he slipped away from the dig site.
Through the ruins.
Past the warning signs.

To the emperor's palace.

Or what was left of it.

The palace was **silent**.
The walls, once **covered in gold**, were now **crumbling stone**.
But as Kai stepped inside—

A whisper echoed through the empty halls.

"You should not be here."

Kai's heart **slammed** against his ribs.
He turned sharply—**no one was there**.

Just the ruins.
Just the throne.

And on the throne's **cold, cracked surface**—

The same symbols that were on the coin.

Kai took a deep breath.
He placed the coin onto the throne.

The room trembled.

The air **shimmered**.

And before his eyes—
A **shadowy figure** appeared.

A man in **royal robes, eyes burning like embers**.
The Golden Emperor.
And for the first time in centuries,

He spoke.

The Emperor's Truth

The shadowed figure stepped forward.
His eyes burned **golden**, but his face was unreadable—a **memory trapped in time**.
Kai **held his breath**.

This isn't possible.

Then, the emperor spoke.

"You hold my final wish."

Kai's fingers **tightened** around the coin.
"Your wish?" he whispered.
The emperor nodded, his voice **calm, but heavy**.

"I ruled with strength. With power. My people feared me—some say they loved me."

His expression darkened.

"But history is written by those who survive."

Then, **the ruins around them changed.**
For a moment, Kai wasn't standing in a broken palace.

He was inside a memory.

The emperor's past.

The throne room was **alive**.

Guards stood at attention. Gold reflected off the walls.
A royal advisor kneeled before the emperor.

"Your enemies grow restless, my emperor. What shall we do?"

The emperor's face was **stone**.

"If they rise against us, they will fall beneath us."

The scene **shifted**.
A garden at dusk.
A woman—**his wife**.
A small boy—**his son**.
The emperor bent down, pressing a coin into his son's palm.

"One day, this will remind you of who we are."

The boy **smiled**.
For the first time, the emperor's expression **softened**.

The memory faded.
Kai was back in the ruined palace.
The emperor's eyes **glowed softly**.

"Now you see me as I was. Ruthless to some. Devoted to others."
"A ruler… and a father."

Now Kai had a choice.

The Choice of a Lifetime

Kai's hands trembled.
The emperor's words echoed in his mind.

"If you keep the coin, my story will live forever. But if you return it, my soul will rest."

This is it.
This is the choice that will decide everything.

Kai stared at the coin.
It was more than metal.
It was a **ruler's final legacy**.
A father's last gift.
A wish left behind, waiting to be answered.
But now that Kai had seen the emperor's past—

Did he deserve to be remembered?

The emperor was powerful. Ruthless. A man who ruled with strength.
His enemies feared him, but his family loved him.
Some would call him a tyrant. Others would call him a protector.

So what was the truth?

Kai's pulse **raced**.

If he kept the coin—**history would remember him.**
But at what cost?

If he returned it—**his soul would finally rest**.
But would that mean **erasing everything he was?**

What do I do?

Kai took a deep breath—
And made his choice.

A Wish Laid to Rest

Kai's fingers curled around the coin.
The air in the ruined palace felt **heavy. Waiting.**
The emperor's shadowy figure stood before him.

"What will you choose?"

Kai took a deep breath.
The emperor was neither fully good nor fully evil.
He was simply… human.

A ruler who had made choices. Some **harsh**. Some **just**.
A father who had once held his son's small hands in his own.
A man who wanted to be **remembered**.

But **not all legacies need to be written in stone**.

Some belong in the hearts of those who will never forget.
Kai lifted the coin—
And gently placed it back onto the throne.

"You already live in history."
"Now… rest."

The emperor's golden eyes softened.
For the first time, he smiled.
His form began to **fade**—slowly, peacefully—
And the moment he vanished, so did the coin.

The ruins were silent once more.
Kai let out a breath he hadn't realized he was holding.
The choice had been made. The past would stay buried.
But as he turned to leave, he looked back one last time.
The throne was empty—
Yet, in the fading sunlight, Kai swore he saw **the faintest shimmer of gold.**
Like a whisper of what once was.
Like a ruler finally at peace.
Kai smiled.
And stepped into the future.

*** The End ***

About the Author

Belinda Chavremootoo tells stories spun from forgotten wishes and secret gardens, where lost coins whisper, and quiet hearts discover their roar.

She writes for both the young and the young-at-heart—tales of wonder, mystery, and magic that shimmer just beneath the surface of the everyday.

When she's not writing, you'll find her in her garden, where tomatoes grow beside thyme, and her two cats keep watch with noble seriousness (and no patience for plot holes).

She believes every soul holds a story worth telling—and sometimes, all it takes is a curious coin or a tiny, talking ladybug to help it find its way home.

May your pockets always carry stories.

Acknowledgements

To the storytellers who came before me, and the readers who keep the stories alive.

To the dreamers, the quiet ones, the kids who whisper to stars and the grown-ups who still believe in magic—this book is for you.

Thank you to my family and friends for the encouragement, the coffee, the "you're still writing?" faces, and the unwavering love.

To my two cats—plot gremlins, keyboard heaters, and midnight meowers —you've truly earned executive producer credits.

And to you, reader:
Thank you for stepping into these tales. For holding lost coins, chasing whispers, and remembering what others forgot.

You are the magic.

Each coin in the stories holds something special—memories, wishes, or magic.

- If you had your own magical coin, what would it carry?

- In "*The Ghost Coins*," Theo learns that some things (and people) don't want to be forgotten. Why is remembering so powerful?

- *"The Chamber of Lost Wishes"* shows a wish with consequences. Do you think some wishes should stay ungranted?

- Nova hears a whisper from the stars in *"The Coin That Fell from the Stars."* Have you ever felt like the universe was trying to tell you something?

- *"The Vanishing Coin"* is about finishing someone else's story. What story would you want to finish or pass on?

- In "*The Emperor's Last Coin,*" Kai has to choose between remembering history or letting it rest. What would you have done—and why?

- Which character or story stayed with you the most? What would you ask them if you could?